KW-484-349

In the **Beginner Reader** level, **Step 9** builds on the sounds learned in previous steps and introduces new sounds and their letters:

igh   ear   air   ure

Special features:

Phonically decodable text builds reading confidence

Short sentences with simple language

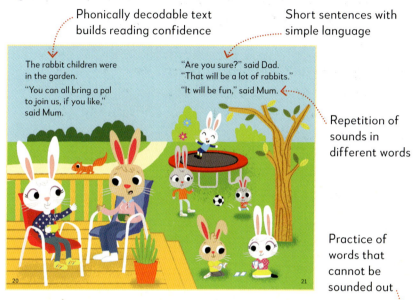

The rabbit children were in the garden.

"You can all bring a pal to join us, if you like," said Mum.

"Are you sure?" said Dad.
"That will be a lot of rabbits."
"It will be fun," said Mum.

20   21

Repetition of sounds in different words

Practice of words that cannot be sounded out

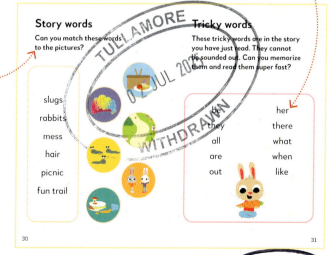

Story words

Can you match these words to the pictures?

slugs
rabbits
mess
hair
picnic
fun trail

Tricky words

These tricky words are in the story you have just read. They cannot be sounded out. Can you memorize them and read them super fast?

he   her
they   there
all   what
are   when
out   like

Summary page to reinforce learning

30   31

TULLAMORE
0 2 JUL 20
WITHDRAWN

OFFALY LIBRARIES

Ladybird

Educational Consultants: Geraldine Taylor and James Clements
Phonics and Book Banding Consultant: Kate Ruttle

LADYBIRD BOOKS

UK | USA | Canada | Ireland | Australia
India | New Zealand | South Africa

Ladybird Books is part of the Penguin Random House group of companies
whose addresses can be found at global.penguinrandomhouse.com.

www.penguin.co.uk   www.puffin.co.uk   www.ladybird.co.uk

 Penguin
Random House
UK

First published 2020
This edition published 2024
001

Written by Dr Christy Kirkpatrick
Text copyright © Ladybird Books Ltd, 2020, 2024
Illustrations by Kevin Payne
Illustrations copyright © Ladybird Books Ltd, 2020, 2024

The moral right of the author and illustrator has been asserted

Printed in China

The authorized representative in the EEA is Penguin Random House Ireland,
Morrison Chambers, 32 Nassau Street, Dublin D02 YH68

A CIP catalogue record for this book is available from the British Library

ISBN: 978-0-241-56437-0

All correspondence to:
Ladybird Books
Penguin Random House Children's
One Embassy Gardens, 8 Viaduct Gardens, London SW11 7BW

The Camping Trip

Written by Dr Christy Kirkpatrick
Illustrated by Kevin Payne

The big rabbit children were off on a camping trip.

"I have never been in a tent at night!" said Clair.

I am sure to get some pics.

7

Bob was too little to go with them. He felt sad.

His ears went high in the air.
Now he was bigger.

Can I go on
the trip?

Dad sat near Bob.

"You are still too little," said Dad.

It's not fair!

Bob and Dad went down
the stairs.

Bob sat in a high chair.
He and Dad began to cook.

"A hot bun is sure to help you
feel better!" said Dad.

Bob spots a bright light in
the next room.

Mum had set up a camp
just for Bob!

This little rabbit had the best night ever!

Story words

Can you match these words
to the pictures?

light

ears

camp

chair

stairs

Tricky words

These tricky words are in the story you have just read. They cannot be sounded out. Can you memorize them and read them super fast?

he	have
was	some
you	were
said	little

What a Sight!

Written by Dr Christy Kirkpatrick
Illustrated by Kevin Payne

The rabbit children were in the garden.

"You can all bring a pal to join us, if you like," said Mum.

"Are you sure?" said Dad.
"That will be a lot of rabbits."
"It will be fun," said Mum.

Dad was right. It was clear there were a lot of rabbits!

Bella and her pal set up a fun trail. There were a lot of slugs!

I have a big fear of slugs!

Clair took her pal up to her room.

That hair is a fright!

Sam went with them and
got a fright, too.

Mum and Dad laid out a picnic for ten rabbits . . . and a pair of slugs!

27

When they went back in,
it was Mum and Dad's
turn to get a fright.

"Just look at this mess!"
said Mum.

Dad let out a big sigh.
"What a sight!"

Story words

Can you match these words to the pictures?

slugs

rabbits

mess

hair

picnic

fun trail